DREAMWORKS

GABBY'S DOLLHOUSE

Meet the Kittycorn

Adapted by Gabhi Martins

DreamWorks Gabby's Dollhouse © 2023 DreamWorks Animation LLC. All Rights Reserved.

All rights reserved. Published by Scholastic Inc., *Publishers since 1920.* SCHOLASTIC and associated logos are trademarks and/or registered trademarks of Scholastic Inc.

ISBN 978-1-338-88539-2

10 9 8 7 6 5 4 3 2 1   23 24 25 26 27

Printed in the U.S.A.   40

First printing 2023

Book design by Salena Mahina and Two Red Shoes Design

Scholastic Inc.

Look, a new Kitty Cat Surprise Box, and it's covered in rainbows!

Inside is a sweet new friend. She's part cat, part unicorn. She has a rainbow heart on her forehead!

There are bells in the box too. I wonder what those are for. And there's a note. It reads, "Every time a rainbow appears, a kittycorn family gets their special kittycorn baby. This is baby Kico."

I know who can help us take care of her until a rainbow appears. Time to get tiny!

"Hi, Kico! I'm Gabby, and this is Pandy Paws. We love your rainbow horn!"

Then Kitty Fairy arrives. She is excited to meet Kico.

"Hey, Kitty Fairy!" says Pandy Paws. "Do you know why Kico's box came with bells?"

"You bet I do! When the rainbow appears, ring these bells so Kico's mom and dad can meet her on top of the rainbow!" Kitty Fairy replies.

Purr-rific! While we wait for Kico's parents, we can show her around the Dollhouse!

"Come back when the rain stops," Kitty Fairy adds. "Then we'll find your special rainbow!"

Uh-oh! Kico is a little nervous about going down the slide.

"The slide is paw-tastic—you have to try it!" Pandy Paws says. Then he has an idea. "What if Kico goes in the middle?"

Kico loves the suggestion!

Ready? Slide time! Whee!

We go to the kitchen and introduce our new friend to Cakey Cat.

"A real kittycorn in my kitchen?! Sprinkle party!" Cakey celebrates.

Kico's hungry, so Cakey makes a rainbow fruit kebob! Kico loves it. She's so happy she starts to kick around. But the kitchen is too small for a baby kittycorn to play!

I'll call Carlita. She can help us!

"Welcome to the playroom!" Carlita says. "Wait until you see what I made for you, Kico! It's the Over-Under-and-Through obstacle course!"

Kico jumps over the giant balls, ducks under the blocks, and leaps through the hoops. But she stops at the dark tunnel.

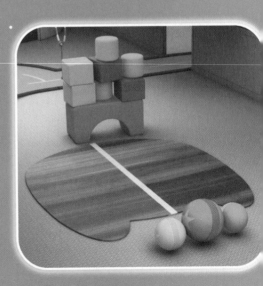

"Sometimes, if you're nervous about something new, it helps to do it with a friend," I tell Kico. "Do you want me to go with you?"

Kico licks my cheek. She wants me to ride on her back!

We're speeding through the obstacle course, but the last hoop is really high . . .

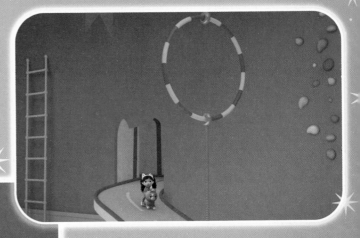

"You can do it, Kico! I believe in you." I rub Kico's rainbow heart to encourage her.

It gives her extra flying powers! Paw-tastic!

Kico flies so high that she knocks a bucket of rainbow chalk over her head.

"Silly Kico. To the bathroom to get clean!" Pandy Paws announces.

Today's the day Kico is going to meet her parents, so it's a very special occasion.

"What you need is one of MerCat's bubble-licious bubble baths!" MerCat smiles.

To make Kico look extra cat-tastic, MerCat makes a special braid with the rainbow bells. Now Kico is ready to meet her parents!

Before we leave, CatRat comes in to say hi to Kico.
"I heard you're waiting for a rainbow," he says. "The
rain has almost stopped. And when the rain stops . . ."

"It's rainbow time!" Pandy Paws and I shout together.

"We better go back to the Fairy Tail Garden," I say.

CatRat is right about the rain stopping.

Kitty Fairy heads toward us when we get to the garden. "Hi, everyone! What a jingle-rific braid, Kico!"

"Kico is ready to meet her parents," I say. "Now we just need to look for the rainbow."

"I have just the thing to help—my Rainbow-Finder!" Kitty Fairy says.

We look for the rainbow side to side, down, and . . . up! There it is!

Kico jingles her bells to call her parents. We see her mom and dad on top of the rainbow!

"Today was so much fun, Kico!" Pandy Paws says.

We hug Kico, and she gives us kisses. It's time for her to go meet her parents!

Kico charges forward and jumps up. Oh no, she can't reach the rainbow!

What are we going to do to help Kico?

Oh, I remember how we can help!

I rub Kico's rainbow heart, and her extra flying powers kick in. Now she can jump cat-tastically high!

She leaps up onto the rainbow and finally meets her forever family! She sends us kisses that turn into hearts!

"Bye, Kico!" we all say. "We'll never forget you!"

DREAMWORKS

GABBY'S DOLLHOUSE

One rainy day, a baby kittycorn arrives at the Dollhouse! Everyone pitches in to take care of Kico until she can meet her family. What fun things will they do together?

PO# 5100763 03/23
Retain for future reference.

Made in the U.S.A.

Scholastic Inc., 557 Broadway
New York, NY 10012

Cover Design by Salena Mahina

SCHOLASTIC
scholastic.com

Look for more DreamWorks *Gabby's Dollhouse* books at a store near you!

FREE DOWNLOAD
TÉLÉCHARGEMENT GRATUIT

Download on the **App Store**

GET IT ON **Google Play**

Télécharger dans l'App Store
Disponible sur Google Play

GabbysDollhouse.spinmaster.com

3+

$5.99 US / $7.99 CAN

ISBN 978-1-338-88539-2

50599

9 781338 885392